The Robin

The
Gums

The
Skiers

The
Riverbank

The
Possum's Tail

My
Burrow

The Snow Wombat

The Snow Wombat

Susannah Chambers

illustrated by Mark Jackson

ALLEN&UNWIN
SYDNEY · MELBOURNE · AUCKLAND · LONDON

Snow on the stockman's hut.
Snow on the crows.

Snow on the woollybutt.
Snow on my...

Snow on the mountain peak.
Snow on the gums.

Snow on the robin's beak.
Snow on my...

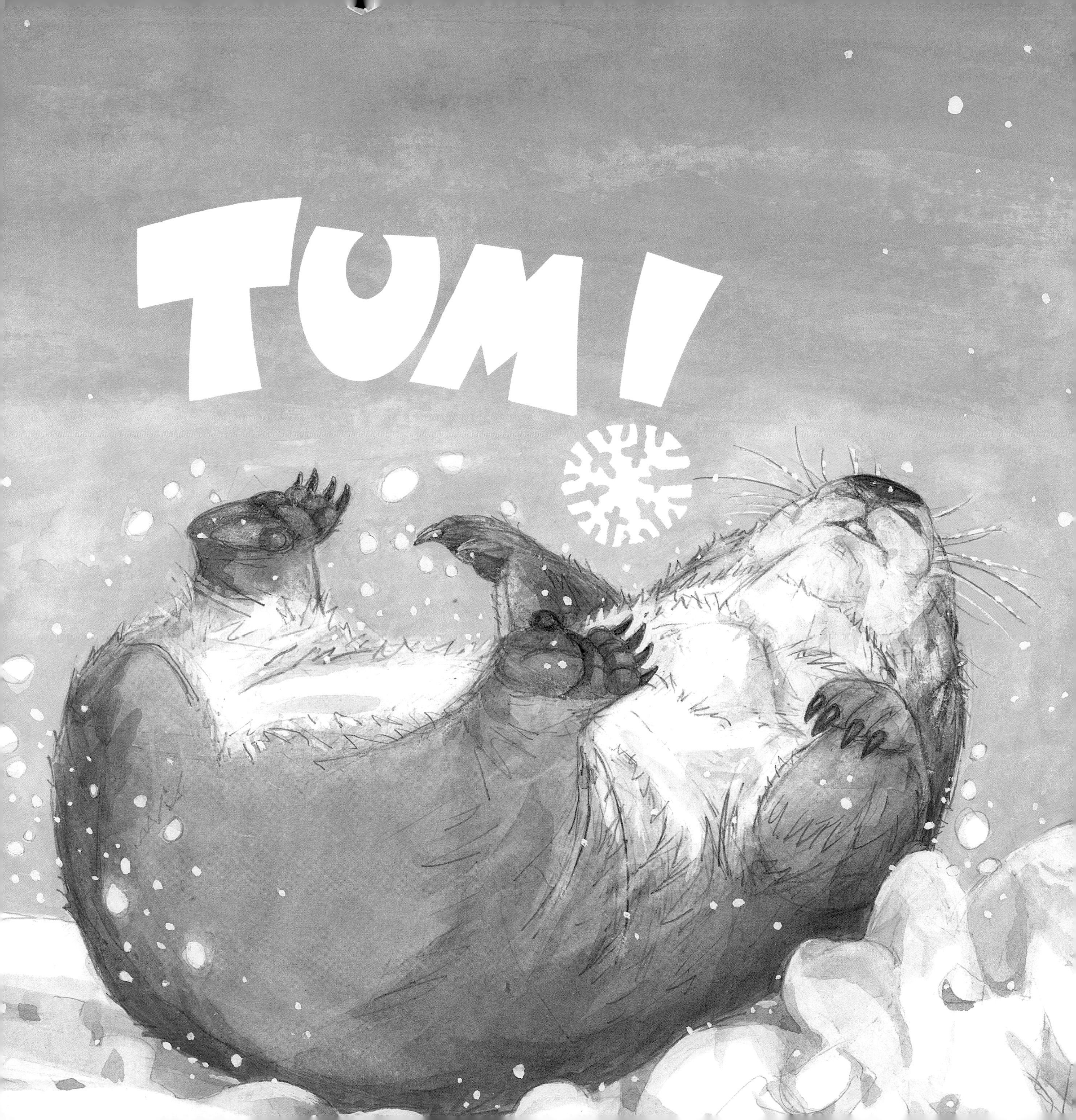
TUMI

Snow on the riverbank.
Snow on the skiers.

Snow on the horses' flanks.
Snow on my...

Snow on the possum's tail.
Snow in the air.

Snow, wind, ice, hail.
Snow...

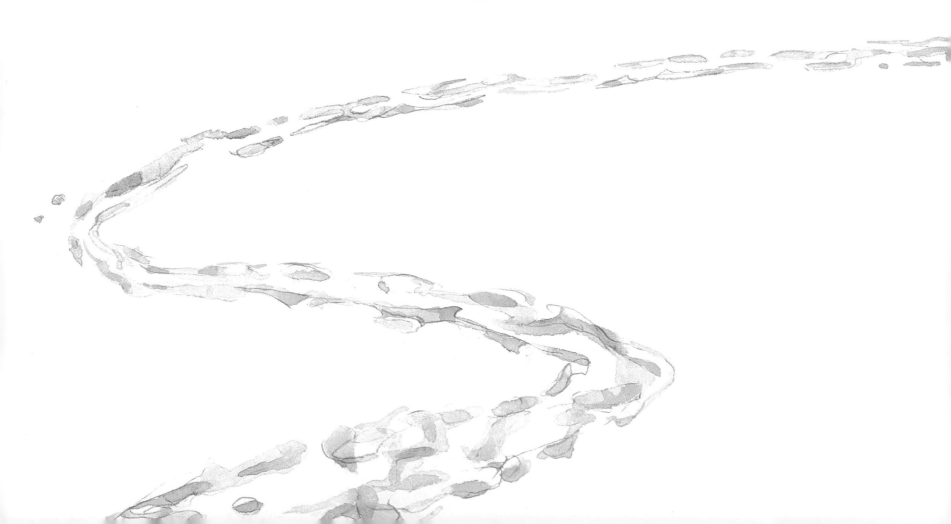

EVERY

WHERE!

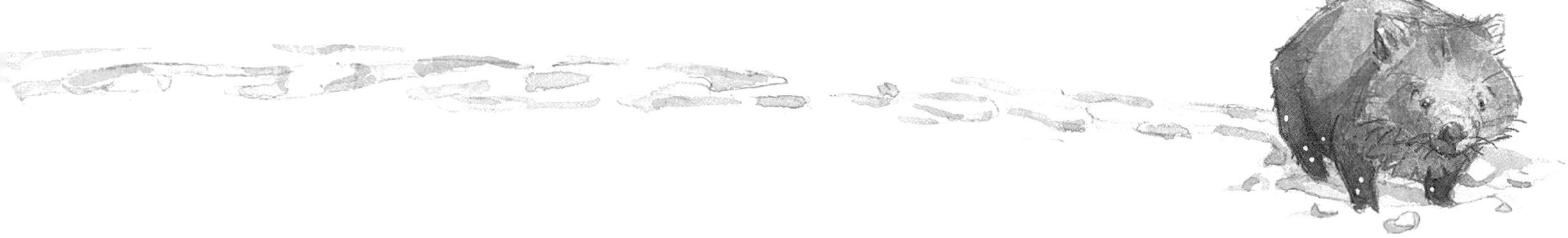

No snow in my burrow.

No snow warm and deep.

No snow when I snuggle in.

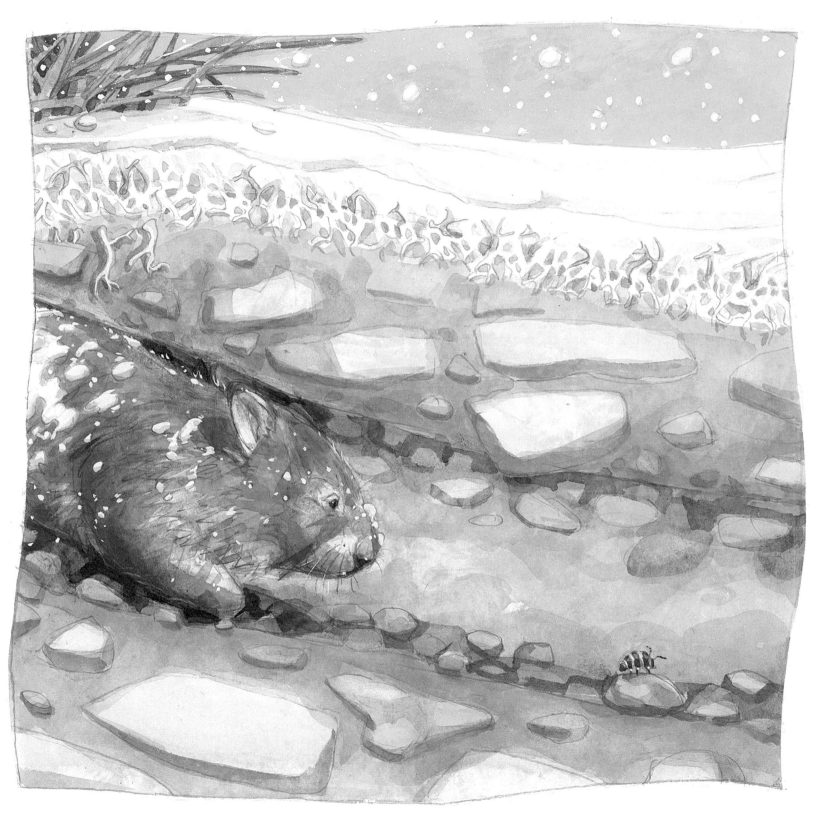

Now I can...

SLEEP.

With thanks to Peter V and the staff at Bayside Libraries. —MJ

First published by Allen & Unwin in 2016

Allen & Unwin – Australia
83 Alexander Street, Crows Nest NSW 2065, Australia
Phone: (61 2) 8425 0100
Email: info@allenandunwin.com
Web: www.allenandunwin.com

Allen & Unwin – UK
c/o Murdoch Books, Erico House, 93-99 Upper Richmond Road, London SW15 2TG, UK
Phone: (44 20) 8785 5995
Email: info@murdochbooks.co.uk
Web: www.allenandunwin.com
Murdoch Books is a wholly owned division of Allen & Unwin Pty Ltd

A Cataloguing-in-Publication entry is available
from the National Library of Australia
www.trove.nla.gov.au.
A catalogue record for this book is available from the British Library

ISBN (AUS) 978 1 76011 381 0
ISBN (UK) 978 1 74336 843 5

Cover and text design by Sandra Nobes
Set in 24 pt Century Schoolbook
Colour reproduction by Splitting Image, Clayton, Victoria

This book was printed in November 2015 by Hang Tai Printing Company Limited, China

1 3 5 7 9 10 8 6 4 2